THE OUTFIT #5

PERIL IN THE MIST

Robert Swindells

D1396131

AWARD PUBLICATIONS LIMITED

ISBN 978-1-78270-057-9

Illustrations by Leo Hartas

Text copyright © 1993 Robert Swindells
This edition copyright © 2014 Award Publications Limited

First published by Scholastic Ltd 1993
This edition published by Award Publications Limited 2014

Published by Award Publications Limited,
The Old Riding School, The Welbeck Estate,
Worksop, Nottinghamshire, S80 3LR

www.awardpublications.co.uk

14 1

Printed in United Kingdom

CONTENTS

PERIL IN
THE MIST

CHAPTER 1

IF YOu SAY IT QUICK

"Now then, you two." Farmer Denton looked up from his copy of the *Lenton Echo*. It was teatime and he was reading at the table, which Mrs Denton reckoned was rude. His two daughters looked across at him. "What is it?" asked Jillo.

"Well – you're forever looking for something to do, aren't you – you and the boys?" The boys, Mickey and Shaz, were his daughters' best friends. In fact the four of them, together with Mickey's dog Raider, were a sort of gang. The Outfit, they called themselves, and they'd shared quite a few adventures.

Jillo nodded. "Anything's better than boredom, Dad."

"Right," agreed Titch. "Anything." At seven she was the youngest member of The Outfit, unless you counted Raider, who was four.

The farmer smiled. "That's what I thought, so listen to this." He read aloud from the piece which had caught his eye.

"Janice Donaldson aged five, pictured here, is a bright, lively little girl. She is also very seriously ill. Her parents are Jim and Molly Donaldson of Shiffley Road, Lenton. A tearful Mrs Donaldson told our reporter, 'Janice suffers from a rare disorder which can be cured by a special operation. There's only one surgeon performing this operation and he's in Hungary. Jim and I want her to have it, but we've been told it'll cost five thousand pounds, not counting such things as airfares and hotels. With my husband out of work we can't possibly get hold of a sum like that. It breaks our hearts to know there's this chance for our little girl and we can't give it to her.' The *Echo* can reveal that the Lenton Community Association has taken Janice's case on board and is looking for ways to raise money. Any organization or individual with a fundraising idea should contact the Community Association Secretary on Lenton 4287."

Mr Denton stopped reading and looked up.

"Why don't the four of you get together and think up a fundraising scheme? I'm sure you'd come up with something if you put your minds to it, and it's a *very* worthy cause."

Jillo nodded. "It is, isn't it? That poor little kid." She looked at her sister. "What d'you reckon, Titch – a job for The Outfit, or what?"

Titch's eyes shone. "I think you're right, Jillo. Five thousand isn't much if you say it quick, and anyway, there's *nothing* The Outfit can't do. I vote we get the others *now* and start thinking."

Within five minutes Jillo had phoned Shaz, and he and the two girls were converging on the caravan at the edge of Weeping Wood, where Mickey lived with Raider.

CHAPTER 2

A GREAT WIFE

Mickey was taking curtains from his washing line when the sisters arrived. Raider rushed to greet them, fussing round their feet as they crossed the clearing towards the caravan. Mickey glanced round. "Come here, you barmy mutt!" he growled. "Hi girls. Wasn't expecting *you* tonight."

Jillo laughed. "Caught you doing the domestic bit eh, Mickey? You'll make somebody a great wife."

"Knock it off, will you? Men gotta keep their place decent too, y'know." Mickey's mother had left when he was small, and his dad was away a lot. Jillo smiled. "I know. Just kidding. We want to talk to you about something important, Mickey. We phoned Shaz. He's on his way."

"OK. Let me get rid of this lot." He carried the curtains into the caravan. It was a warm May evening so the girls sat on the step, where Mickey joined them. Raider looked into the trees, growling softly, and after a moment Shaz appeared. "What's going on?" he demanded. "You sounded very mysterious on the phone, Jillo."

"Come sit down," said Titch, "and we'll tell you."

Briefly, the two girls told the story of Janice Donaldson. When they'd finished Shaz said, "*I* know something we could do."

"What?" asked Mickey.

"Sponsored walk."

"Boring. *Everybody* does them, Shaz. People must be fed up of sponsoring flipping walkers."

"I'm not talking about your *ordinary* walk," protested Shaz. "I'm talking about *endurance* walking. I'm talking the *Five Moors'* walk."

"What the heck's that when it's at home?" demanded Jillo.

"It's this walk in North Yorkshire. Forty miles. You walk across five moors and four valleys and end up at the sea."

"Or dead," growled Mickey. "Forty miles is

a long, long way, Shaz old son. Titch'd never make it, for a start."

"I'd make it if *you* did, you plonker!" cried Titch.

"People do it all the time," said Shaz. "Kids too. One guy *ran* it."

"Yes – and think of the dosh," said Jillo. "Fifty sponsors, fifty pence a mile each – that's a *thousand quid*."

"Oh sure!" chuckled Mickey. "First catch your fifty rich sponsors."

"Well, *I* think it's worth mentioning to the Community Association," said Shaz. "I'll do the phoning if you like. What d'you say?"

Jillo nodded. "I reckon we should, Shaz."

"Me too," growled Titch. "Then watch me walk that loud-mouthed curtain-washing Mickey right into the ground."

Mickey shrugged. "OK – seems I'm outvoted." He grinned. "And don't worry, Titch – when you keel over after the first three miles, your uncle Mickey'll give you a piggyback the rest of the way."

CHAPTER 3

ADULTS SPOIL EVERYTHING

"Lenton 4287 – Mrs Parfitt speaking."

"Oh hello, Mrs Parfitt. I've got a fundraising idea for that little girl."

"The Janice Donaldson Appeal?"

"Yes."

"Lovely. Will you tell me your name?"

"Oh, yes – sorry. It's Shazad. Shazad Butt."

"And how old are you, Shazad?"

"Ten."

"Tell me about your idea."

"Well, it's not just mine, Mrs Parfitt. There's four of us. Five if you count Raider."

"Did you say *Raider*, dear?"

"Yes. He's Mickey's dog."

"Ah! I – didn't I read a piece about you and your friends in the *Echo* some time ago – something about a kidnap and an old house?

What do you call yourselves – The Firm – something like that?"

"The Outfit."

"*That's* it. I remember now. Go on, Shazad."

"Well – there's this walk, see? The Five Moors Walk. It's in North Yorskshire. We thought we'd have a go at doing it. It's forty miles. We'd get people to sponsor us for so much a mile, so we'd raise money even if we didn't manage to finish."

"Hmmm. Have you *been* to North Yorkshire, Shazad?"

"No. I read about the walk in a magazine."

"Well, I've been there, and it's wild country. The idea of the four of you tackling the moors alone makes me uneasy."

"We can do it, Mrs Parfitt, honestly. The Outfit can do *anything*."

"You may *think* that, Shazad, but *adults* die on those moors. Fit, experienced adults sometimes. Your idea's a very fine one and I'm reluctant to let it go, but I think we have to adapt it a bit. Get some older people involved, perhaps. There's the Scout troop for a start. Look – leave it with me, Shazad. Give me a ring tomorrow when I've had a chance to talk to some people. Will you do that?"

"Ah … OK, Mrs Parfitt, but I don't know what the others will say. The Outfit usually works by itself 'cause adults *spoil* everything."

"Goodbye then, Shazad, till tomorrow. Thank you for calling."

"OK. 'Bye."

CHAPTER 4

GING-GANG-FLIPPIN'-GOOLIE

Next day was Saturday. The friends met as usual at Outfit HQ – a roomy, wooden building in a corner of one of Farmer Denton's fields. Outfit HQ had a stove, a long table and some chairs. There was a kettle for brewing tea, a rug on the floor and a basket by the stove for Raider. On the door was a notice: *HQ The Outfit – no admittance.*

"OK, Shaz," said Jillo when they were seated round the table with mugs of tea. Raider had his own chair but he didn't care for tea. "Let's have your report."

Shaz pulled a face. "You're not going to like it. I spoke to Mrs Parfitt – she's the Secretary – and she thought the idea was great, but…"

"But what?" demanded Mickey.

"Well … she doesn't think we should tackle

the walk by ourselves."

"We won't *be* by ourselves," said Titch. "We'll be together."

"Yes, I know, but she's talking about *adults*. Thinks there should be adults along. And she mentioned the Scout troop."

"The *Scout* troop?" Mickey hooted. "I'm not doing any sponsored walk with a bunch of Boy Scouts going Ging-gang-flippin'-goolie all over the place, and as for *adults* – it'd be like a school trip. You know – don't do this, be careful of that. Might as well take your flippin' granny. And anyway, it's *our* idea. Why should other people muscle in?"

"Yeah," nodded Titch. "We do it ourselves or we don't do it – that's what *I* say."

"Now just a minute," put in Jillo. "Aren't we forgetting something?"

Mickey looked at her. "What are you on about?"

"Janice Donaldson, that's what I'm on about, Mickey. The kid we're supposed to be doing it for. If her folks don't get that five thousand, she *dies*. What does it matter who we walk with, as long as we raise the dosh? *I'll* walk with Count Dracula and Frankenstein's monster if it'll save that kid's life."

Mickey looked down. Everybody was quiet for a while. Finally Shaz broke the silence. "Jillo's right. All that matters is the kid. Let me call Mrs Parfitt at teatime, huh? See what she's fixed up, if anything. And whatever it is, let's do it for little Janice, OK?"

"OK," murmured Titch.

"Yeah, all right," growled Mickey, "let's do it."

"Yip!" went Raider, and their laughter broke the tension.

CHAPTER 5

WATCH THE ECHO

"Mrs Parfitt ... it's Shazad Butt. You said to phone." It was six o'clock. Shazad was calling from home.

"Yes, Shazad, I was waiting for your call. I've spoken to various people about your idea. Everybody thinks it's a good one and several would like to be involved, including the vicar."

"The *vicar*?"

"Don't sound so surprised, young man. He's a great one for walking, our vicar. He'd like to come along and so would his daughter, Jane. Mr Craven the Scout leader is interested. too: in fact he's undertaken to organize the whole thing."

"But, Mrs Parfitt – it's *our* idea. I feel like it's being taken away from us and I know my friends'll feel the same."

"I understand Shazad, really I do, but nobody's trying to take it away from you. Everyone I spoke to said what a brilliant idea it was, and how clever the four of you were to think of it, but you see an expedition of this sort needs to be organized. There are a thousand things to be considered ... transport, equipment, food and water, communications, first aid. You need a support party with a vehicle. Letters have to be written to the Five Moors Club, so that those who complete the walk within twenty-four hours can receive their Five Moors badges, and to the Fell Rescue Service so they know the party's departure and expected arrival times. It takes experience to set up a thing like this, Shazad, and Mr Craven and the vicar have years of experience between them."

"Hmmmm ... so what happens first?" asked Shaz. "I mean, how does it all get started?"

"There'll be a meeting at the village hall. I don't know when yet – Mr Craven's fixing that up, but it'll be soon. Everybody interested in the walk will be at that meeting. Watch the *Echo*: there'll be an announcement about it. All right, Shazad?"

"I … I guess so, Mrs Parfitt. It's got a lot bigger than we intended, that's all."

"Ah, but you see, Shazad, the bigger it is the more money it'll raise, and that's what counts, isn't it?"

"I suppose so."

"Of *course* it is. And think about this: however much it raises, it'll all be thanks to The Outfit. That's something to be proud of, you know."

"Yes. Thanks, Mrs Parfitt. We'll watch the *Echo*, then. 'Bye."

"Goodbye, Shazad. I look forward to seeing you and your friends at the meeting."

CHAPTER 6

RELATIVES DON'T COUNT

It was Farmer Denton who spotted the notice. It was Tuesday teatime and he was reading at the table again. "Here it is, girls," he said. "*Walk in aid of Janice Donaldson Appeal. Public meeting. village hall, Lenton, Thursday 11th May at 7.30. All welcome.*"

"Is that it?" asked Jillo. "Is that all it says?"

"What d'you *want* it to say?"

"Well – I thought it'd say Five Moors Walk, forty miles, something like that. I mean, it could be a stroll round the park, couldn't it?"

Her father chuckled. "Everybody *knows*, sweetheart. The Scouts took a note home and the vicar made an announcement from the pulpit. It's the talk of the village."

"Well, I don't like it," grumbled Titch. "It was better when it was just The Outfit."

The farmer looked at her. "If it was just The Outfit, Matilda, you wouldn't be doing it. Neither of you. Do you really think your mum and me would have let you go swanning off across the Yorkshire Moors by yourselves?"

"We'd be all right. The Outfit's done harder things."

"Not with our blessing, it hasn't," said Mrs Denton. "I'm *thankful* it's going to be a proper, organized expedition with adults to keep an eye on you. I want to help that little girl as much as the next person, but I wouldn't want to lose my own children doing it."

After tea the two girls made their way to Outfit HQ. The boys hadn't arrived yet so Titch and Jillo got the stove going and put the kettle on. It was just coming to the boil when Shaz and Mickey arrived together. Mickey waved a copy of the *Echo*.

"Seen it, have you? The notice?"

Jillo nodded. "Dad read it out. Thursday. Sounds like the whole village'll be there."

"I know. Old Latimer mentioned it in class today. She's *going* would you believe, and so's her husband, who must be about ninety.

If we've to go at *their* speed it'll be Christmas when we reach the sea."

"What I want to know," murmured Shaz, "is, if everybody's going on the walk, who's going to do the sponsoring? Do we sponsor each *other* or what?"

Jillo laughed. "Everybody's not going, you turkey. There's people in Lenton can't make it down the *chippy* without a car. Even so..." She smiled. "I vote we start asking people *now*. After Thursday *loads* of walkers'll be going round asking."

"I've started," grinned Shaz. "Grandad's promised me twenty pence a mile." Shaz's parents were on a long visit to Pakistan, so his grandad was looking after him.

"Us too," said Titch. Mum and Dad are giving *us* twenty pence a mile."

"Relatives don't count," growled Mickey.

Jillo chuckled. "Just 'cause you haven't *got* any relatives, Mickey."

"I've got my dad. He'll sponsor me, no trouble."

"Where *is* he though?"

"I dunno do I, but he'll show up. He always does."

"OK." Jillo looked at the others. "Relatives don't count so we'd better get a move on. We don't have sponsor forms yet so we'd better stick to people who know us."

"Like who?" asked Shaz.

Jillo shrugged. "Postman. Milkman. Teachers. Shopkeepers. People who *know* us."

Titch looked at her. "Do we go together or what?"

"In two's, Titch. You come with me." She looked at the boys. "We'll make it a competition, right? Who gets most sponsors. We stop at dusk, count up at school tomorrow. OK?"

Mickey shrugged. "Fine." He grinned. "Me and Shaz gonna win easy with our secret weapon."

"What secret weapon?"

"Raider. We knock on a door and when someone answers we say, quid a mile or we have this dog put down. People're so *crazy* about animals it can't fail."

Raider cocked his head on one side and gave his master a reproachful look. Mickey bent and scratched the lurcher's ears.

"Barmy mutt," he said. "Can't you take

a joke?"

"Yip!" went Raider. He was only a dog, but he knew Mickey loved him. Who could ask for more?

CHAPTER 7

NEVER MIND FORTY

The girls won the competition because the name Denton was well-known in the village – the family had farmed there for generations. They got twenty-two sponsors. Shaz and Mickey didn't mind. They got fourteen, which was better than they expected. Everybody they spoke to thought the expedition was a splendid idea, so that by Thursday evening the four were quite happy that Mr Craven and the vicar had taken it over. As for Raider, he didn't care *who* was going to be in charge as long as there'd be plenty of rabbits for him to chase.

Hundreds of people were at the meeting. They sat in rows on stacking chairs facing the platform. On the platform was a long table and behind the table sat five people. The children gazed at them. They knew the vicar of course, and Mr Craven, and Linda Fellgate the reporter, though they were puzzled as to why she was on the platform. The other two – a woman and a man – were unknown to them. The vicar kept glancing at the clock. At half past seven he nodded to somebody at the back, who closed the doors. The vicar smiled at the rows of faces.

"Good evening, ladies and gentlemen, and welcome. It's good to see so many villagers emulating the Good Samaritan by coming to the assistance of their neighbour, when it might be so much easier to pass by on the other side. I'm going to begin by introducing my four colleagues, though I'm sure some of you know *all* of them, and that all of you will know *some* of them." He looked to his left. "The gentleman at the end is Mr David Craven, leader of the Lenton Scouts. Next to him is Mrs Parfitt, who is, of course, Secretary of the Lenton Community Association, which brings us to me. I'm Henry Melford, whom a *few* of you may have met at St Sulpice where I'm vicar." A ripple of laughter. "On my immediate right is Mr Jim Donaldson, father of little Janice." Murmurs of sympathy and surprise in the audience. "And last but by no means least, journalist Ms Linda Fellgate, who is here representing the proprietors of the *Lenton Echo*."

The four spoke in turn. The Scout leader used an overhead projector to show a map he'd made of the Five Moors Walk. He talked about the ruggedness of the terrain and the changeable nature of the weather. He hoped many members of the audience would join the expedition, but warned that only physically fit persons who possessed the right equipment should consider doing so. He'd run off some lists of equipment, and intending walkers would be given a copy, together with a sponsor form and a sketch-map of the route, when they came to sign up.

Mrs Parfitt said the response to the appeal for fundraising ideas had been overwhelming. A number of events were being organized, and those villagers who didn't feel they could help with the walk would no doubt find one or other of these to their liking *and* within their capabilities.

Linda Fellgate sprang the surprise of the

evening when she revealed that her employers intended to donate one hundred pounds for each walker who completed the trek. This brought a burst of applause, during which Mickey leaned over and whispered to Titch, "I wonder if that includes Raider?"

"'Course it does," Titch replied. "It says each *walker*, not each *human*."

When Jim Donaldson stood up, everything went still. He talked quietly about his daughter – how she was just like any other little girl, except she was in and out of hospital all the time. How brave she was, because she was always laughing even though she seldom felt well, and that when she grew up she was going to be a nurse. You could tell he was nearly crying when he said that, and when he whispered that without the operation there'd be one nurse fewer in the world he *was* crying, and there were sniffles in his audience, too.

Jillo, hanky in hand, whispered, "I'd do every inch of that walk now if it were four hundred miles, never mind forty."

"Me too," choked Mickey, and the others nodded because it's hard to talk when you're crying.

CHAPTER 8

TICKLIST

"Crikey!" gasped Titch as the four left the hall with their sponsor forms and lists. "All this stuff, and we've only got till Saturday."

Jillo scanned her form. "It's a *week* on Saturday, you turkey. Nine days from now – we've bags of time."

"Mr Craven told us that," said Shaz. "He said we're doing it then because it's the first weekend of the Spring Holiday and we'll have a week to recover before school. You obviously weren't listening."

"I wish it *was* this Saturday," said Mickey. "I can't wait to have a crack at it."

"Well, you'll have to," said Jillo, "so let's talk about something useful, like how we're going to kit ourselves out."

With new sponsors to track down and their equipment to assemble the eight days passed quickly, and Friday evening found the four at Outfit HQ, checking their kit. Four rucksacks stood open on the table. Mickey was working his way down a ticklist of essentials, and the others were packing items away as he read them out. Jillo was packing Mickey's rucksack as well as her own. As each item was stowed, Mickey ticked it off. When he reached the bottom of the list, the four had everything Mr Craven considered necessary for tackling the Five Moors Walk. Raider, bored with these complicated preparations, had gone off to practise his rabbiting.

"Phew!" Mickey straightened up and dropped his pencil on the list. "All present and correct, at long last. Thanks, Jillo. I suggest we split now – get an early night." He smiled. "No kip at all tomorrow night, remember – just a three-hour break. I'll see you outside the village hall at half eight, and don't forget your stuff."

They trooped out, dangling their packs. The sun was a hazy orange, low over Weeping Wood. "Looks like we'll have a good day for it," said Titch.

" 'Course we will," grinned Shaz. "We're The Outfit. It wouldn't *dare* rain on us."

CHAPTER 9

THE MORE THE MERRIER

It was cool but dry when the friends met next morning. Two coaches stood by the village hall and the pavement was chock-a-block with men, women and children in plaid shirts, warm trousers and boots. A driver was heaving rucksacks, map-cases and walking sticks into the baggage hold of his coach while David Craven stood by its open door with a clipboard, ticking off names as people clambered aboard. Most of the walkers were adults, including Venture Scouts and Guides. Raider seemed to be the only dog. The vicar, strikingly un-vicarlike in his bulky kit, was checking people on to the second coach. Behind the coaches stood the support team minibus laden with soup and tea, plastic containers of water and stoves to heat it on, spare clothing, first aid and medical gear.

The nurse from the health centre was in charge of the minibus, which would rendezvous with the walkers on each of the three roads they would cross during the trek. Any walker who became ill, blistered or exhausted need only make it to the next rendezvous to receive treatment. He or she could then elect to drop out of the walk and stay with the support team till the expedition was over.

"Wow!" gasped Mickey. "Two coachloads. That's more than a hundred people."

"Great," nodded Jillo. "The more the merrier."

"Yeah," said Shaz, "but I hope we get seats together."

They did. The expedition was supposed to leave at eight forty-five but there were so many people and so much gear that it was after nine when the two coaches pulled away from the kerb, leaving a scatter of well-wishers waving in a haze of blue exhaust, and headed north for the village of Acaster where the Five Moors Walk began.

CHAPTER 10

THIS TIME TOMORROW

The first part of the ride wasn't particularly interesting and anyway Shaz had the window seat, so Mickey studied the sketch-map on the back of his kit list. A dotted line showed their route between Acaster and the coastal village of Saltick where the walk would end. They'd trek uphill on to Acaster Moor and cross it, then drop down into a valley with a road running along it. That was where they'd meet the support team for the first time. It was nine miles from Acaster to this road. Mickey twisted round in his seat. The two girls were sitting behind.

"Hey, Titch." He tapped the map. "You've only to survive nine miles and nurse'll change your nappy and cuddle you the rest of the way."

"Huh!" Titch's nose wrinkled in scorn.

37

"If you and Raider swapped brains we would have an intelligent conversation, and if you swapped faces as well, Raider'd be the world's thickest, ugliest dog."

Mickey chuckled and turned around. After the road came Roseberry Moor. He frowned. *That* name rings a bell, he thought. Isn't that where…? "Hey, Shaz."

"What?"

"Look." He smoothed the map across his knees and pointed. "Roseberry Moor, see?"

"Yeah – so what?"

"Well, I've been there. Couple of years ago, with Dad. There's a stone circle. Roseberry Circle it's called."

"Well it would be, wouldn't it?"

"Shut your face and listen. It's dead spooky, right? Haunted, my dad says, by the spirits of the humans sacrificed there by the Druids three thousand years ago."

"Oh, sure. We'll see 'em then won't we, sometime this aft?"

"Dunno. It's not on the map. Maybe we don't go near it."

"So why go on about it?"

Mickey shrugged. "I fancy seeing it again,

that's all."

"Ask Mr Craven if we'll be near it."

"He's on the other bus, you turkey."

"When we get off."

Mickey pored over the map. Stony Rigg Moor, Limber Hill Moor, Wheeldale Moor. We'll see the sea from Wheeldale Moor. All downhill from there. This time tomorrow we'll be trogging into Saltick, then it's home and bed for us and Hungary for little Janice Donaldson.

No danger.

CHAPTER 11

DON'T BE FOOLED

"Right, listen up, everybody." They'd disembarked, collected their gear and walked through the village to where the road became a track that meandered uphill. Raider, who'd spent the journey under Mickey's seat, kept dashing up the slope and back again, keen to be off. Mickey called him to heel and turned to listen to the Scout leader, who indicated to the track.

"This is it, folks – the start of the Five Moors Walk. As you can see it's a well-defined path and it's like this pretty much all the way, but don't be fooled. It may look like a nice Saturday afternoon stroll, but the terrain, once you stray from the track, is rugged and dangerous. There are boggy areas, peat hags and potholes. In some places there are nineteenth-century mineshafts, some of them unmarked, so it's vitally important we stick to the track at all times." He nodded towards the slope. "Acaster's the smallest of the five moors so we've got a nice, easy start. It's only nine miles from here to the B497 in the next valley, but again, don't be fooled. The second moor, Roseberry, is thirteen miles across with a long, steep pull to the top. So," his eyes swept the walkers' rapt faces, "if anybody feels bad after this first stage – blisters, stitch, breathlessness, anything at all, they should think seriously about staying with the minibus. Is that OK – any questions?"

Mickey stuck up his hand. "Will we see Roseberry Circle at all, sir – when we reach Roseberry Moor, I mean?"

The Scout leader shook his head. "No – er – what's your name, lad?"

"Mickey, sir."

"No, Mickey, we won't. The track passes within half a mile of the stones but you can't see them because of a fold in the hills. Any other questions? No? Right." He grinned. "I clocked us out at 11.55, so if we're going for the badge we've got till 11.55 tomorrow to

reach the post office at Saltick. Are we going for the badge, folks?"

Their roar of affirmation hit the hillside and bounced back as an echo. They shouldered their packs and strode on to the slope. The Janice Donaldson Five Moors Walk Expedition was under way.

CHAPTER 12

PROBABLY NOTHING

They paused at the top of the slope for a breather and to let the stragglers catch up. Some of the walkers eased off their packs and sat down. Jillo looked back. Acaster was a Lego village in the valley. She turned. The moor lay before her, an undulating patchwork of blacks and greens which faded in the distance, merging with the sky so that there was no horizon.

The vicar, who'd volunteered to bring up the rear, shepherded the last pair of walkers on to level ground. The Scout leader motioned him over and the two conferred. Mickey, sitting on a tussock chewing a grass-stem, stared across at them. "What's up with them two, d'you reckon?"

Shaz shrugged. "Planning the next bit, I suppose."

"Vicar looks worried," murmured Titch.

"Hey up," said Jillo, "he's gonna say summat."

"Listen up folks, please." He waited till he had everybody's attention. "It's probably nothing – a bit of heat-haze perhaps – but David and I don't like the look of that sky ahead. We'd a good forecast this morning but they don't always get it spot on, so we're keeping an eye on it. If it starts to rain – and I'm talking about *hard* rain – so early in the expedition, we may have to decide whether or not to press on." Groans from some of his listeners. He smiled. "As I said, it's probably nothing, but it pays to be cautious on the hills. We'll move on now. Stay together as much as possible, please. Let's go."

They strode on, watching the sky. The haze remained, but they didn't seem to get any closer to it. The sun was pleasantly warm, the peaty track as springy as an expensive carpet underfoot. Somebody up front started singing *The Happy Wanderer*. Mickey groaned, but others joined in and soon everybody was swinging along to the rhythm, the threat of rain forgotten. Song followed song, so that when the terrain began falling away and they saw the road snaking between the meadows in the valley below, it was hard to believe they'd covered the best part of nine miles.

When they reached the road the minibus was there. Raider got a bowl of water. Everybody else had tea or juice. The nurse treated a couple of blisters but nobody dropped out, which the vicar said was excellent. It was good sitting in a line at the roadside, sipping tea and scanning the slope they'd soon be tackling. One down, four to go. A breeze had sprung up, rippling the long grass like waves on the sea. Mickey drained his plastic cup and wiped his mouth with the back of his hand. "If we stop anywhere up there for a breather," he said, "we're dodging off to see the stone circle, right?"

"Yip!" said Raider, who'd seen it before.

"D'you think we *should*?" asked Shaz.

Jillo shook her head. "No. We're supposed to stay together."

"We'll *be* together, won't we?" grinned Titch. "The Outfit, I mean. We don't need anybody else."

"OK folks," called the Scout leader. "Break's over. Time to move on." Groaning good-

46

naturedly they straightened their stiff limbs, shrugged on packs, surrendered their litter to support team volunteers and crossed the road. The daunting escarpment of Roseberry Moor loomed, seeming to touch the sky as they waded through buttercups at the foot of the slope.

CHAPTER 13

FOUR AGAINST ONE

The climb seemed never-ending. It separated the fit from the less fit so that by the time the leaders were half-way up, the expedition was strung out over a quarter of a mile. Nobody talked. Every ounce of effort was going into putting one foot before the other. Only Raider was unaffected – dashing up and down the slope, snuffling tussocks, yipping and wagging his tail. Jillo amused herself watching Titch, who hadn't forgotten Mickey's taunt about nappies and cuddles and was busting a gut to stay ahead of him. Little by little The Outfit moved closer to the head of the line, overtaking their red-faced, perspiring elders till only David Craven and his Scouts were in front. When the four friends reached the top and looked back, they found a two-hundred-yard gap between themselves and the next group, and the stragglers were dots of colour almost half a mile below. Shaz, grinning, raised both arms in the air. "Ask me who's one hundred per cent fit, then."

"The Outfit, that's who," panted Titch, who'd beaten Mickey by a whisker. David Craven smiled across at them. "Well done, you four. If I were you I'd sit down till the others catch up – you've earned a rest." The Scouts had shed their packs and collapsed into the needle grass where they lay gazing at the sky. The Outfit followed suit except for Raider, who had picked up the scent of a rabbit and gone bounding off.

"Wish I had his energy," grunted Jillo.

It was twenty minutes before the vicar delivered the hindmost knot of walkers to the summit, and the Scout leader allowed these unfortunates fifteen minutes to recover before the expedition pressed on. By this time a stiffening breeze had drawn a veil of mist across the sun, and as they moved off a fine drizzle began to fall. There was a delay of several minutes as the walkers unpacked cagoules and overtrousers and struggled into them. The vicar and David Craven conferred with many skyward glances, but the walkers muttered and shook their heads, making it clear that nobody wanted to quit, so the decision was taken to press on. They walked with their heads down, listening to the crackle of their waterproofs and the faint hiss of the rain upon them.

Up front, the Scout leader talked into his radio, reporting to the support party on weather conditions and visibility. The rain wasn't getting any heavier but the mist was closing in, blown by a wind which felt colder than it had lower down. The organizers had scheduled a lunch stop roughly halfway across the moor, at a spot where an outcrop of boulders afforded some shelter. The expedition reached the outcrop at 5.10 p.m. They were well behind schedule, but the Scout leader knew the walkers must eat something or risk running out of energy. He held up a hand.

"OK everyone – lunchtime." Cheers greeted his words. He grinned, swiping droplets from his lashes with the back of his hand. "Get in the lee of the rocks and huddle down. We were supposed to stay here for an hour, but because we've fallen behind schedule and in view of the weather, I think we'll cut it to twenty minutes. I'll call the minibus – reschedule our rendezvous for 7.30. Anyone unhappy with that?"

Nobody was. They found overhangs and hunkered down in groups, unpacking flasks and sandwiches. It felt warm out of the wind, and the walkers munched and chatted cheerfully enough in spite of the surrounding gloom. Raider smelled lunch and came lolloping back, shaking his drenched coat over the four friends before taking his share of their food. They'd finished eating and were sipping hot tea when Mickey said, "I remember these rocks. I saw 'em when Dad brought me to the stone circle. There's a bit of a track somewhere, leading to it." He pointed. "I think it's over that way." He drew back an elasticated cuff to peer at his watch. "We've got seven minutes. Who's coming?"

"Seven minutes?" cried Jillo. "You can't do a mile in seven minutes, you turkey."

"Sssh!" Mickey glared at her. "Not so loud, for Pete's sake. I didn't say we *could* do a mile in seven minutes, did I?" He looked at the others. "We don't have to. The track we're on's dead easy to follow, right, so what if the others *have* moved on when we get back? Well soon catch up – look what happened on that slope." He grinned. "The circle'll be dead spooky in this mist, so who's game and who's chicken?"

"Well I'm not chicken," asserted Titch.

Mickey smiled. "You're game, then. What about the rest of you?"

"I still think we should stick with the party," said Jillo.

"We will," hissed Mickey, "as soon as we've had a squint at the circle. We're only talking about a few minutes, Jillo."

"I'll come," volunteered Shaz. He looked at Jillo. "That's four against one, counting Raider."

Jillo sighed, biting her lip. "Well – I suppose if you're *all* going…"

"Good lass!" Mickey began gathering foil and bits of eggshell, stuffing the litter in his rucksack. "Better make it snappy then." He peered all around. "And keep low – we don't want old Craven spotting us, or the vicar."

"If anybody says anything," whispered Titch, "we just say we're off to spend a penny."

Mickey chuckled. "Titch," he grinned, "you're a genius, though I say it myself. Come on."

CHAPTER 14

SOMETHING MOVED

The track was just about where Mickey had said it would be. They were walking into the wind, which meant the rocks were between them and the party and nobody saw them go. The track snaked downwards, and when Jillo glanced back the outcrop was no longer in sight. "I hope we can find our way back," she murmured.

"'Course we can," Mickey assured her. "I told you – I've done it all before."

The wind had strengthened, driving drizzle like needles into their cheeks. "I think there's ice in this rain," gasped Titch.

"Never!" laughed Mickey. "It's *May*, you turkey, not December."

"She's right though," put in Shaz. "Look at Raider's coat."

53

They looked and saw tiny specks of white, hundreds of them, caught up in the lurcher's wiry hair. "That's not ice," said Mickey, "It's old age. Raider's going grey, aren't you boy?"

"Yip!" confirmed Raider. They laughed and trudged on.

It took eight minutes to reach the circle. "The others moved on a minute ago," said Jillo.

"Give up moaning," growled Mickey. "Look at this – worth coming or what?"

It *was* worth coming. There were sixteen standing stones. The circle was so wide that those farthest away were faint shadows in the mist. The four children stood gazing at the circle, wondering what bloodthirsty rituals had been enacted here centuries ago. No wraiths glided between the ancient stones, but they could feel they were not alone. There was no doubt in anyone's mind that presences hovered here, unseen. Even Raider was subdued, crouching at Mickey's feet. He gazed whimpering into the circle with bristling hackles, watching something humans cannot see.

Titch gulped and whispered, "I think we ought to go."

Shaz nodded. "Yeah." The wind made keening noises round the stones. Mickey pointed. "Look. Over there."

They looked. It was hard to be sure with ice on their lashes: it might have been nothing but a shred of windblown mist, but *something* moved. *Something* emerged from between two stones, glided across the circle's open space and vanished into the whirling sleet.

"Come on," hissed Jillo. "The others're a mile away by now."

"My dad was right though, wasn't he?" whispered Mickey. "It *is* haunted. You all saw it, didn't you?"

Jillo nodded. "Yes Mickey, we saw it. Now can we get back, please? The others…"

"Are a mile and a quarter away by now," interrupted Mickey. "We *know*."

"Well, it *is* important," flared Jillo. "I don't suppose you've noticed, but it's actually snowing, and I can hardly see my hand in front of my face."

"That's because you haven't got your hand in front of your face."

"No, but you know what I mean."

It *was* snowing. They'd been too spellbound

to notice, but the weather had got a lot worse in the last few minutes. The mist was thicker, the wind more fierce, and snow was beginning to settle. They must hurry or it would obliterate the track and they'd be lost.

CHAPTER 15

HEADCOUNT

"Folks." The wind boomed among the boulders and the Scout leader had to shout to make himself heard. "As you can see, conditions are approaching a white-out. I've just spoken to our support party, and it seems the Countryside Warden at Stony Rigg is strongly advising that we get off the tops as quickly as possible. I'm afraid that since we're not quite halfway to our rendezvous, that means turning back. It isn't snowing in the valleys and the minibus will meet us on the B497, staying with us till the coaches arrive. It's bitterly disappointing I know, but I'm sure you all appreciate how extremely foolish it would be to continue in the teeth of the advice we've received. If I could ask you to line up on the track and stand still for a minute we'll do a quick headcount.

Thank you."

They counted together, then separately, then again, and the result was the same each time. Four missing. The Scouts trudged round the outcrop, shouting hello and peering into the cracks and overhangs. Nothing. A woman approached the vicar. "It's those children isn't it – the ones whose idea this was? They had a dog with them."

"Ah yes, of course." The vicar hurried across to the Scout leader. David Craven frowned. "Hmmm – one of 'em asked about Roseberry Stone Circle, didn't he? I wonder ... Paul! Darren!" The two Venture Scouts trotted over. "You two stay with me." He turned to the vicar. "Set off back, Henry, please. This stuff's melting as soon as it hits the ground – it shouldn't obliterate the track. Keep 'em moving, and we'll catch you when these kids turn up."

The party turned and began to retrace its steps. David Craven gazed after it for a moment, then took his two companions in a half-circle round the outcrop and on to the almost-vanished track which led to the circle.

CHAPTER 16

FIGURES IN THE MIST

"Admit it, Mickey," panted Jillo. "The track's gone. We're lost."

"Are we heck. Listen. On our way to the circle we were walking into the wind, right?"

"So?"

"So if we keep the wind behind us, we're bound to be heading back the way we came."

"Yeah, but we might not be on the track."

"Doesn't matter. As long as we're going the right way, we'll hit the Five Moors' path eventually. Come *on*."

The wind seemed to help a bit as they slogged uphill. They were all scared except Raider, but none of them was going to admit it. Being a dog, Raider had no idea anything was wrong. They were together, and it would take more than a bit of rough weather to stop *him* rabbiting. As his friends dragged their boots through the slushy mire, the lurcher made excited dashes to the left and right, often disappearing for minutes at a time. There *were* rabbits – he could smell them – but they would take some finding.

It was during one of these forays that Raider spotted three figures in the mist. They were human, and therefore of no interest to him. He crouched in the sodden grass and they passed without seeing him.

CHAPTER 17

ONLY THE WIND

"There's the circle, sir. No sign of 'em."

"Hmmm. You two cast about a bit. Footprints. Anything. I'll give 'em a shout."

The Venture Scouts walked slowly among the stones, peering at the ground. Their leader cupped his mouth with his hands and called, "Halloooo! Is anybody there?" He stood on a tussock and peered all around. "Halloooo – give us a yell if you're out there." He strained his ears but only the wind replied. Paul and Darren rejoined him.

"Anything?"

"No, sir." Darren shrugged. "Even if they *were* here – just minutes ago – this sleet'd have covered their tracks by now."

David Craven nodded. "You're right. They came here – I *know* they did – but they must've

62

lost the track and they could be anywhere by now. Search around a bit if you like, but for goodness' sake stay together. I'm going to call Fell Rescue."

CHAPTER 18

ARE THEY HECK

"There you go, Jillo – is that the rocks or isn't it?"

Jillo looked where Mickey was pointing. The outcrop loomed dimly to their left. She nodded. "That's it all right, but we weren't on the track or it'd be straight in front." She veered left, heading for the rocks. Shaz and Titch followed her. Mickey hooted.

"What're you going *that* way for? The pathway's here. You'll only have to come back, you dummies."

The trio turned. "I thought the others might be waiting," said Jillo.

"Are they heck," chuckled Mickey. He nodded to his right. "They're a mile away by now, on there. Don't even know they've lost us."

"We'd better catch 'em then," panted Titch. "Don't want to miss the next rendezvous with the minibus."

"Why?" grinned Mickey. "Thinking of dropping out or something?"

"Am I hummer."

"Well come on then."

They turned their backs on the outcrop and strode out. Mud and wind had sapped their strength, but the prospect of hot soup at the minibus spurred them on. The wind, gusting from the right, plastered their waterproof trousers against their legs and flung clouds of stinging sleet across the track. When Shaz looked back, the white-out had swallowed the rocks.

CHAPTER 19

GO FOR IT

"Hey," gasped Shaz, "it's not sleet any more. Just rain."

"That's because we're going downhill," said Jillo. "Have been for a while."

"So we'll be at the road soon?" queried Titch. "We've done Roseberry Moor?"

"Ye-es," murmured her sister. "We've done it, but what worries me is, where are the others? We've been making good time – why haven't we caught up with the stragglers?"

"We will," growled Mickey, "if we stop blethering and save our breath for walking." He pulled up the sleeve of his cagoule and peered at his watch. "It's twenty-five to eight. We are supposed to meet the minibus at half seven, which means the others are down there *now* and we've got twenty-five minutes to catch 'em before they move on again."

"But surely," said Shaz, "they'll do a headcount at the minibus. They did before. Then they'll know we're behind and wait for us."

"I tell you what I think," said Jillo. "I think they chucked it in – decided to call the whole thing off while we were down at the circle. I don't think there's anybody in front of us."

"Don't talk wet!" snarled Mickey. "There's no way they'd jack it in for a bit of sleet. What about the *kid*? If they chucked it in there'd be no dosh and Janice Donaldson'd *die* and it'd be their fault. And anyway they'd have done a headcount, wouldn't they? Found we weren't there and waited for us."

"They *might* have," retorted Jillo. "You wouldn't let us go look, remember."

"Shut your face, Jillo. They're at the minibus right now, towelling their hair and sipping hot soup, and if you fancy a bit of that yourself we'd better get down there before they move on." He glanced at the sullen sky. "If only this rain'd let up. And the wind."

They hit the road at ten to eight. There were no walkers, and no minibus. "Maybe we're at the wrong place?" suggested Titch.

Mickey scoffed. "How can we be, dumbo? We came right down the track."

"Don't take it out on Titch," flared Jillo, "just because you've been proved wrong. The others aren't here because they've never been here, Mickey. They jacked it in, back at the rocks."

"But what about the minibus?" objected Shaz. "Surely…"

"They radioed the minibus, Shaz. It turned back too."

"You don't know that," cried Mickey.

"I know it's not here, where it's supposed to be." She gazed at the bleak, sodden hills, their tops shrouded in mist. "Let's face it Mickey – we're alone. It'll be dark in an hour and we're stuck out here in the middle of nowhere without backup. No grub. No radio. No leader. I don't know what we're supposed to do in a situation like this – follow the road I suppose. It's bound to lead somewhere, eventually, and at least it's not snowing down here."

Mickey looked at her. "And what about the kid, Jillo? If we sling it in, where's the dosh coming from to get little Janice to Hungary?"

Jillo shook her head. "I don't know, Mickey." She sighed. "Look – suppose we went on. Suppose we made it to Saltick. What would we raise? A hundred apiece from the *Echo*, plus our sponsor money. Five hundred. Six if they pay Raider. Nowhere near enough anyway and I've got Titch to think about. Mum and Dad'd never forgive me if anything happened to her."

Titch sniffed. "I'm OK, Jillo. I'm as fit as anyone here, and maybe you've forgotten what you said at the meeting. *I'd do every inch of that walk now it if were four hundred miles, never mind forty.* Remember?"

"Sure I remember, but I didn't know we were going to wind up by ourselves out here, did I?"

"But that was the original idea, Jillo," put in Shaz.

"Huh?"

"It was going to be The Outfit, remember? Just The Outfit. We were cheesed off when loads of other people started muscling in."

She looked at him. "So what're you saying, Shaz – you think we should go on, is that it?"

He shrugged. "Why not? We're in good shape. Two moors behind us, three to go. I vote we go for it."

"That makes two of us," growled Mickey.

"Three," amended Titch, "and Raider makes four."

Jillo looked at them. "OK," she murmured, "I'm outvoted again. It's just that … somebody's probably out looking for us … Fell Rescue or something…"

"Well, that's OK," said Mickey. "They know where we're heading, so they'll know where to look. And anyway, we don't *need* rescuing – we're The Outfit." He grinned. "Ten minutes to spend a penny and we're out of here. What d'*you* say, boy?"

"Yip!" went Raider, to nobody's surprise.

CHAPTER 20

LIKE THE FLIPPIN' M1

Stony Rigg Farm is the highest in North Yorkshire. Its rough, tilted pasture was heather once, and will return to heather as soon as the wiry occupant of the squat grey farmhouse gives up his struggle to raise sheep on the thin soil and retreats with his rheumaticky wife to the valley like everybody else. It was this rheumaticky wife, placing a light in the window to guide her husband home, who saw four small figures slogging in the rain up the track which passed within yards of the farm. Shaking her head and muttering under her breath, the old woman threw a shawl round her bony shoulders and hurried to the gate.

"Evenin'."

Mickey, who hadn't seen her waiting there, jumped. "Oh – er – evening. We're not trespassing, are we?" The four stopped, gazing at the woman. Raider trotted over to sniff the rusted iron of the gate.

"Where you four off this time o'night?"

Mickey smiled. "Saltick."

"Saltick?" Beads of rain sparkled in her thin grey hair as she shook her head. "Saltick's eighteen miles, young man. Across t'tops."

He nodded. "We know. We're on a sponsored walk."

"By yourselves?"

"Er – yes."

She shook her head again. "Mustn't go on. Not tonight. Dark's coming and there's a mist. You'll stray from t'path. There's holes. Old mineshafts. Where've you come from?"

"Lenton."

"Lenton? Well, you won't get back *there* tonight, but there's a bus at nine'll take you as far as Acaster. I'd get it if I was you."

"We can't. There's this kid. She'll die if we don't raise that dosh."

"*You'll* die and all if you try them tops i'the dark. Folks die regular as clockwork up there. I've lived here all my life – seen 'em stretchered down many a time wi' sheets over their faces."

Jillo nodded. "We know you're right, but you see this is something we *have* to do. We promised."

"Aye, well." The old woman gazed at them through watery eyes. "You've been told. Now it's up to you. If my husband was here he'd drag you down to t'bus stop. I can't." She began to turn away, drawing the shawl more closely round her. "Think on," she flung back at them. "Stick to t'path."

"I think we should've listened to her," said Jillo, when they'd left the farm behind. "The mist's getting thicker and the dark makes it worse. What if we stray off the track?"

"How *could* we?" cried Mickey. "It's like the flippin' M1. I could follow it with my eyes shut."

Jillo shrugged and said nothing. They toiled on, and presently the way became less steep and levelled off. Before them, hidden by mist, lay the vastness of Stony Rigg Moor. It was quite dark now, and the rain was still falling. They struck out across the invisible terrain and almost at once, without knowing it, left the track to follow a path which led only to some long-abandoned quarries.

CHAPTER 21

GOOD BOY, RAIDER

It was nine o'clock and pitch black when Raider planted himself barking in the middle of the track, forcing Mickey to stop. The boy, tired and wet and more scared than he'd care to admit, aimed a kick at the animal.

"Get out the flippin' way, you barmy mutt!" Raider dodged the kick and stood his ground, yapping.

"He's telling us something, Mickey," cried Titch.

Mickey shook his head. "He's barmy, that's all."

"I dunno so much," said Jillo. "The track's been getting narrower, Mickey, and there aren't the footprints. Look." She shone her torch on the muddy ground. "I don't think this is the right path at all."

74

" 'Course it is." Mickey stepped off the path to go round the dog. Raider lunged at his ankles. Mickey aimed another kick and strode on, his torch beam jerking over tussocks of needle grass on the marshy ground. He'd got round the dog and was about to rejoin the path when he stopped short with a cry. Two metres in front of him the tussocks stopped on the lip of a yawning gap. Two more steps and he'd have plunged headlong down a sheer rockface into a hole so deep torchlight didn't reach the bottom.

"It … there's a quarry," he croaked. He was

shaking so violently his torch beam jittered about, turning falling rain into shoals of silver fish.

"There's another over here," cried Shaz. "And another, I think. We're *surrounded* by flippin' quarries."

"Well, that settles it," said Jillo. "We're on the wrong path."

"Wh ... what we gonna *do*?" whispered Titch.

"Go back," said her sister. "It's all we *can* do."

"I daren't move," gasped Titch. "What if...?"

Jillo reached for the child's hand and squeezed it. "We're OK on the path, Titch. We didn't run into anything coming down, did we?"

"No."

"Well then."

Mickey returned to the path, looking sheepish in the light from Shaz's torch. Raider had stopped barking and was capering about, tongue lolling. Mickey bent briefly to ruffle the creature's sodden coat. "Good boy, Raider. Good boy." He straightened up. "Back then, eh?"

Jillo shone her light on her watch. "Five past nine. We were supposed to rest from nine to midnight."

"Yeah," growled Shaz. "In fine weather, on the right track. All we can do now is press on."

As the exhausted little party turned to retrace its steps, a team of Fell Rescue volunteers, slogging along the Five Moors' track looking for them, passed the place where the quarry path branched off. It was dark, and the wind flung rain in their eyes, and nobody spotted the footprints left in the mud by four pairs of boots and a dog.

CHAPTER 22

SOMEONE ELSE'S KID

As The Outfit returned to the fork where they'd gone wrong, David Craven, Paul and Darren trudged out on to the road where the minibus was waiting. It was twenty to ten. The coaches had left for home carrying the vicar and the rest of the expedition, leaving the support team scanning the steep side of Stony Rigg Moor in the hope of seeing seven people and a dog. Briefly, the Scout leader filled them in on the fruitless search he'd led, and told them he'd radioed Fell Rescue.

"They've got two parties out," he said, "one from Acaster and one from Saltick. They alerted the RAF but the fog's too thick for a helicopter. The two parties will walk towards each other, covering the whole route, but they say that if those kids have left the track there's virtually no chance of finding them in the dark."

The nurse looked at him. "Can't *we* do something? I mean, surely we don't just pack up and go home, leaving them out there? Can't *we* search too?"

The man shook his head. "I offered, Susan, but the guy in charge at Acaster – the Countryside Warden – said no. What he actually said was, searching moors that are riddled with bogs, quarries and mineshafts is no job for a bunch of amateurs – we'd end up looking for you, too. So what I propose is this. You run me to Fell Rescue HQ in Acaster, then set off home. I'll phone the kids' parents and wait there for news." He sighed and shook his head. "I hope and pray it's *good* news – it must be the most terrible thing in the world to lose someone else's kid."

CHAPTER 23

RATHER SERIOUS NEWS

"Mrs Denton?"

"Speaking."

"David Craven, Mrs Denton. I'm sorry to be calling at this late hour, but I'm afraid I have some rather serious news for you."

"Is ... it's my daughters, isn't it? Jill and Matilda?"

"Yes, it is, but they're not hurt, Mrs Denton. They're not even overdue."

"Then what ... where are you calling from, Mr Craven?"

"I'm at Fell Rescue HQ in Acaster. We had to turn back because of bad weather but four children, including both of your daughters, had slipped away while we were resting – we think to look at Roseberry Stone Circle. We took a headcount before setting off back and discovered their absence. A search-party was dispatched at once to the Circle, but found no trace of them."

"Oh my God. You're telling me they're lost, aren't you? Lost in the middle of nowhere at eleven o'clock at night? Is anyone doing anything about it, Mr Craven? Is anybody *looking* for them?"

"Of course, Mrs Denton. We alerted the Fell Rescue Service at once and they have two parties out, covering the entire route. I feel sure they'll..."

"You're at Acaster, is that right?"

"Yes."

"Wait there. We're coming, my husband and I. We'll..."

"I wouldn't, Mrs Denton, really. I don't think there's anything..."

"What do you expect us to do, Mr Craven? Have some cocoa and go to bed? Is that what *you'd* do if it was *your* children out there?"

"No, it's not, Mrs Denton."

"Well then. We'll be there as soon as we can. 'Bye."

"Lenton 2116, Mr Butt speaking. Who is

calling, please? Ah, Mr Craven. Yes, I am the grandfather of Shazad Butt. What? Shazad is *missing*? And his friends? Who is searching for them, please? Fell Rescue Service? Yes, I see. And where are you, Mr Craven? Acaster. How can I...? No, I have no car but I must come. Shazad's parents are away you see, and I am responsible for him. Yes, I am knowing the Dentons. *Their* car? Yes. I will telephone them immediately. Thank you, Mr Craven. Goodbye."

CHAPTER 24

CARRY YOUR FLIPPIN' GRANNY

"Is it wishful thinking or are we going downhill?" called Shaz from the rear. The wind had moderated a little, making it easier to talk, and sleet had given way to rain. "It's *not* wishful thinking," flung back Mickey. "We've cracked Stony Rigg."

"Hoo-flippin'-ray," growled Jillo. "It feels more like Stony Rigg cracked me."

"No way," grunted Shaz. "One hundred per cent fit, that's you, Jillo."

"Oh sure. What time is it, for Pete's sake?"

Mickey stopped, pulled up his sleeve and shone his torch on his watch. "Seventeen minutes past midnight. I bet you thought it was late, didn't you?"

"It *is* flippin' late," moaned Titch. "Three hours past my bedtime and I'm starving and all."

"We're all starving," said Mickey. "The trick is not to think about food, Titch. Think about Janice Donaldson getting on that plane instead."

"I've *tried*, but I was watching her from the coffee shop at the airport with people munching burgers all round."

"Look at that barmy dog," grumbled Shaz. "Dashing about as if he set off half an hour ago, not twelve hours twenty-five minutes."

Jillo groaned. "Is that how long we've been going? No wonder I'm shattered."

"Are we carrying on?" asked Shaz. "When we reach the road, I mean?"

"There isn't a road, you turkey," said Mickey. "It's a river. Look." He shone his torch on the bedraggled sketch map. "River Usk."

"How do we get across?"

"Bridge."

"Then uphill again, eh? I don't know if I can stand it."

" 'Course you can. And look. Limber Hill Moor's only four miles across. We'll be over in an hour."

"You're kidding yourself," cried Jillo. "We're

not making four miles an hour, Mickey. Two, if we're lucky."

"OK – *two* hours then. That means we'll cross the B491 around half two, then there's only Wheeldale Moor. That's six miles, so at two miles an hour we'll hit Saltick at half five in the morning – just in time to see the sun rise out of the sea."

"What – through this lot?" Shaz indicated the mist, thinning now that they were descending.

"It'll clear," chirped Mickey. "You wait and see."

"It's all right for you," snapped Titch crossly. "You're always staying up all night. You're used to it."

Mickey grinned. "I told you, Titch – Uncle Mickey'll carry ums when ums can't manage any more."

"You carry your flippin' *granny*!" retorted Titch.

They trudged on, their torches making puddles of light on the miry track.

CHAPTER 25

NOT REALLY WARM

The Outfit reached the bridge at half past midnight. If they'd arrived twenty minutes earlier they'd have run straight into the two Fell Rescue parties who'd rendezvoused there at midnight, having covered the whole route. The sixteen men had talked briefly and radioed their respective HQs before piling into two Land Rovers, which had bounced and lurched their way over Wheeldale and Limber Hill Moors, and now roared back over Limber Hill, heading for the B491.

"I can smell ciggies," said Titch as they sat on the low stone parapet, dangling their aching feet over black water. The rain had stopped, but as they were soaked to the skin already it made little difference.

"Can you heck, you dipstick," growled Mickey. A massive blister had formed on the ball of his right foot. He could feel it throbbing, but he daren't take his boot off in case it wouldn't go on again.

"I don't think it's a good idea, stopping," said Jillo. "I was OK while we were moving but I'm freezing now."

"I'm not," said Shaz. "In fact I'm warmer. I could just curl up and fall asleep."

"Yeah, well," said Mickey, "you know what happens to Arctic explorers, don't you? They fall asleep and never wake up again."

Shaz smiled dreamily. "Sounds nice."

"Hey!" Jillo nudged him. "You're not serious are you, 'cause Mickey's right. You're not *really* warm – you just *think* you are." She slid off the parapet, wincing as the soles of her feet took her weight. "Come on – either we move on now or we give up and wait to be found."

"We don't *need* to be found," grunted Mickey. "We're not lost. Come on."

It was hard. Much harder than before. The pause had stiffened their limbs. Their sodden clothes clung to their bodies, draining their reserves of warmth even as the soles of their feet burned. Raider stopped pursuing unseen rabbits and loped doggedly at Mickey's heels with his head down and his tongue out. The wind had dropped and the rain kept off but the mist lay dense on the tops, enshrouding them clammily as they toiled upward through sphagnum bog and reed bed. Mickey's blister burst. He felt the fluid spurt, then his coarse thick sock began to chafe the raw sore with every step, forcing him to hobble. The others had slowed drastically, too, and he knew that Jillo's estimate of two miles an hour had been over-optimistic. He longed to stop – to sink down in the spring heather and close his eyes, and he knew that if he did so he would die. For the first time since they started, Mickey was seriously worried.

CHAPTER 26

NOTHING POSITIVE

The Denton Range Rover turned into the car park at Acaster Fell Rescue HQ and rolled to a halt. It was one a.m. The Dentons got out. Mr Denton turned to help old Mr Butt, who didn't walk very well, and the trio moved towards a lighted doorway in which the Scout leader stood silhouetted. Thirty miles away, their exhausted children were beginning the four-mile slog over Limber Hill Moor.

"Come on in. I am most dreadfully sorry … you must be feeling terrible."

"No more than you, I daresay," said the girls' father gruffly. "Is there any news?"

David Craven sighed. "Nothing positive, I'm afraid. The two teams rendezvoused an hour ago without having found anything. They're on their way here now. Or rather, one party

is. The other's returned to Saltick. They believe
the children have strayed from the track, and
that there's no chance of finding them in the
dark. They'll resume the search at first light."

"So it's a matter of waiting for morning?"

" 'Fraid so."

"Hmmm ... rather be out there *doing*
something myself. Can't we take a vehicle up –
have a look round?"

The Scout leader shrugged. "I can't stop you
if that's what you feel you should do, and of
course I'm more than willing to come along."
He pulled a face. "Fell Rescue aren't keen
though. Amateurs add to the problem seems to
be their view."

"Ah, but it's not *their* kids lost out there.
I think I'll drive over." He looked at his wife.
"Why don't you wait here love – no point both
of us going. What about you, Mr Butt?"

The old man nodded. "I will come with you
if you don't mind, Mr Denton. I cannot rest
here, thinking about the boy's parents – how
they will never forgive me if..."

"Sure. You come along." He looked at David
Craven. "Can't leave Mrs Denton here alone,
David. Will you stay with her till we get back?"

"Of course."

"Right." The farmer strode to the door, holding it open for the old man. "We'll see you later, then."

The door swung shut. The girls' mother stared at it, then slumped forward on her chair and began to sob. The Scout leader laid his hand on her shoulder.

"They'll be fine, Mrs Denton," he murmured. "You'll see." He wished he felt as confident as he sounded.

CHAPTER 27

FAIRY MUSIC

It was only four miles, but Limber Hill Moor seemed to go on for ever. Jillo had developed blisters, and she and Mickey hobbled along behind Shaz and Titch with Raider out in front, hunting in a half-hearted way. He kept vanishing into the mist where their torchlight couldn't penetrate, reappearing minutes later from another direction. It seemed the five of them were the only walking creatures on the moor. Even the rabbits were asleep.

"A burrow," murmured Jillo. "A nice, dry burrow with a soft warm floor. I'd sleep and sleep and sleep…"

"Aw, knock it off will you?" groaned Mickey. "It's bad enough without that. Surely we've done four flippin' miles by now?"

"Not unless we're lost," said Titch over her

shoulder. "Want me to carry you yet, *Uncle* Mickey?"

"Shut your face, Titch, or I'll tear your arm off and beat you to death with the soggy end."

"Hey, listen!" Shaz stopped, his head cocked on one side.

"What is it, dunderhead – fairy music?"

"No, listen. It's a motor. We must be near the road."

They listened, and Shaz was right. Somewhere, not far away, a vehicle was growling through the night.

"Sounds like a truck," whispered Mickey, taking care not to let the others see how relieved he felt.

"Wish I was in the back of it," yawned Titch, "fast asleep."

"Oooh, don't," moaned Jillo. "You're as bad as me with my nice warm burrow."

"Well, at least it means we've done Limber Hill," said Shaz. "Four down, one to go."

"Oh Lord!" groaned Mickey. "I don't know about that, Shaz old son. We've given it our best shot but it's four in the morning and we're done in. Maybe it's time to call it a day."

"Is it heck!" cried Shaz. "I'll tell you what

it's time for. The *oath*. You know? The Outfit oath."

"Oh, come *on*, Shaz. That's all we need right now – form a flippin' circle and leap about in the middle of the night."

"I don't mean form a circle, you donkey. Chant and walk's what I'm on about. Like U.S. Marines. Good for morale. Lifts the spirits and all that."

"My spirits sloped off about three hours ago," moaned Mickey, "taking my morale with them." He sighed. "Go on then – can't make things any worse, can it?"

Shaz began and they joined in one by one, matching the chant to their pace. It came out a bit sluggish, but it did seem to make them feel better:

"Faithful, fearless, full of fun,
Winter, summer, rain or sun,
One for five and five for one –
THE OUTFIT!"

And that's how they marched to the road.

CHAPTER 28

POSTWoMAN PAT

At the roadside they peeled off their cagoules, spread them on the banking and sat on them. Their sweaters were still damp so they changed them, pulling on the spares from their packs. Jillo produced a slab of Kendal Mint Cake, broke it up and passed round the pieces. They closed their burning eyes and munched the candy.

"You know," said Mickey, "we were supposed to rest for three hours back on Stony Rigg but we never did. I reckon we should do it now."

"In three hours," grunted Shaz, "it'll be seven a.m. Wheeldale's six miles across so that'll take us another three hours, which means we'll arrive in Saltick around ten. So." He grinned. "We'll easily qualify for our badges."

"I'd rather qualify for ten hours in a feather

bed," mumbled Titch.

Mickey nodded. "Me too, kiddo, but this bank's better than walking. I'm off to sleep." He unlaced his boots, eased them off, ordered Raider to guard them and lay back with a sigh. Titch lay down too. Jillo got up and went behind a bit of a wall to do a pee. Shaz wrapped his arms round his knees and gazed along the road. After a minute Jillo came back and lay down. Shaz and Raider kept watch.

Shaz was dozing with his forehead on his knees when he heard a growl from Raider, then a motor. He looked at his watch. Just after five. A pearly luminescence glowed through the mist. It was getting light. Looking up he could just make out the rim of Wheeldale Moor against the eastern sky.

Raider growled again. A postman's van came round a nearby bend. Jillo stirred and opened her eyes. "What's happening, Shaz?"

"Postman Pat."

"Huh?" She sat up, knuckling her eyes. "Oh crikey – we should hide."

"No time." Shaz watched the van. Maybe he'll ignore us, he thought, but the van was slowing. It pulled over just before it reached them. A window came down and a woman stuck her head out.

"What the heck're you kids doing here at this hour."

"Resting," said Shaz.

"Yes I can see that, but why are you here? Where've you come from? She frowned. "You've not *escaped* from somewhere, have you?"

Shaz laughed. "Nothing like that. It's a sponsored walk. The Five Moors. We've come from Acaster."

"By yourselves?"

"Well ... we didn't *start* by ourselves, but we lost the others. We think they turned back."

"I should think they *did*, in yesterday's weather. Why didn't you?"

"Oh, well you see – we're The Outfit." By this time Mickey and Titch were awake and sitting up. "We *never* turn back. And besides there's this little girl – Janice Donaldson. She has to go to Hungary for an operation and we're raising the dosh for her fare."

"Ah-ha." The woman opened her door and got out. "So you've still got Wheeldale to do?"

"Yes."

"Hmmm. And are you all right? I mean..."

"We've got blisters," said Mickey. "And we're absolutely starving. Apart from that and being dog tired, we're fine."

"Well…" She smiled. "I can't do anything about tiredness unless you want a lift, but there's two flasks of coffee and a pack of sandwiches in the van if they'll help, and I *might* be able to do a temporary job on the blisters."

"Magic," grinned Mickey.

The woman nodded towards the bend she'd just rounded. "There's a bit of a lay-by just round that bend. I'll reverse into it if you can walk that far."

The woman's name *was* Pat, and over the next half hour they drained her flasks, ate all her sandwiches and had their wounds bound. All that was missing was the black and white cat. By the time they said goodbye, waving as Pat's van roared away in a cloud of exhaust, they were feeling one hundred per cent better. It was daylight, the mist was thinning and they were only six miles from the sea. What they didn't know was that while Pat had been attending to their needs, Farmer Denton's Range Rover had crossed the road and gone bouncing up the track to Wheeldale Moor.

CHAPTER 29

SPANGLES ON THE SEA

Old Mr Butt leaned forward to peer through the mud-spattered windscreen. "I think … do you see *men*, Mr Denton, there at the foot of the slope?"

The farmer nodded. "I see them, Mr Butt." He steered the bouncing vehicle round a pothole. "Walkers. Might have a word – ask 'em to keep their eyes skinned." He'd stopped the Range Rover several times on the moor, and the two men had peered into the mist, calling their children's names. Now they were in sight of the sea, heading for the Fell Rescue Centre at Saltick, hoping for news.

When they reached the walkers, Mr Denton braked and stuck his head out of the window. Before he could speak, a man in an orange cagoule stepped forward. "Mr Denton?"

"Er – yes. How did you know?"

The man stuck out a hand. "Pete Garside, Fell Rescue. Acaster radioed … said you might show up. No luck then?"

"No. Can't see a thing up there. Mist."

The man nodded. "It's due to clear. We're off now, and a helicopter'll join us as soon as there's enough visibility."

"OK if we tag along?"

"Well … better not sir, if you don't mind." He looked at the farmer, then at the old man in the passenger seat. "I wouldn't worry – the kids'll be all right. They've got all the right gear with them. Find 'em in five minutes likely, once the chopper comes."

"I hope you're right, Mr Garside. Is there someone at the Centre?"

"Oh aye. Brews a good cuppa, young Stanley does." He tapped the handset clipped to his belt. "We're in touch. You'll know as soon as—"

"What is that?" Mr Butt leaned towards his half open window, one hand cupped behind his ear.

Garside looked at him. "What is it, sir?"

"Singing. Someone is singing."

"Singing?" He cocked his head on one side. "I don't hear anything, sir."

"It's coming and going. You must listen hard."

Everybody listened. At first there was only the mew of a gull and the distant shush of the sea but presently, rising and falling, fading and returning but quite unmistakably now, came the sound of young voices raised in song. Twelve pairs of eyes scanned the hillside. There was movement. There *was*. Way up there, where the mist began. Shadows. Two shadows. No, three. Four? As the watchers strained their eyes four small figures, bent under packs, came tottering out of the haze.

"Hey, look!" Titch pointed downhill to where tiny figures clustered round a vehicle. "Somebody's expecting us."

"Yeah, well." Mickey grinned as a warm glow ignited in his heart, expanding. "Let's show 'em how The Outfit comes home." They straightened their aching backs, lifted their heads and belted out:

"Ging-gang goolie goolie goolie goolie watcha, ging-gang-goo, ging-gang-goo. Ging-gang..."

Raider, sensing their jubilation joined in. "Yip-yip..."

"Yooray!" cried The Outfit, so loudly that a startled gull went wheeling away where the sun cast spangles on the sea.

CHAPTER 30

MEGA!

"They've come!" Shaz stood in the doorway of Outfit HQ brandishing a padded envelope. The others eyed it.

"What's come?" asked Titch.

"Our badges. Little white skulls with a five on them. There's a certificate too, to prove we're members of the Five Moors Club."

"Mega!" cried Jillo. "We can put it on the wall next to our pictures."

Two weeks had passed since the five had hobbled proudly into Saltick. After sleeping the clock round, they'd endured a richly deserved telling-off from the Countryside Warden, who'd told them they might have died through sneaking away to the Circle. They'd been cheered too, though – cheered and clapped and photographed and interviewed by Linda

Fellgate, who'd done a full page for the *Echo* about their exploits. Now their woes were forgotten, their blisters healed. In faraway Hungary, Janice Donaldson was making good progress after her operation. There'd been snaps of her in all the daily papers, smiling in the little nurse's uniform her carers had given her. They'd cut them all out and pinned them on the wall, together with a moving letter from the child's parents.

The *Echo* had been as good as its word, donating a hundred pounds for each of the four walkers plus a hundred for Raider. Every sponsor had paid up smiling, including all of those whose walkers had turned back, and an anonymous well-wisher had sent a cheque for a thousand pounds "as a token of my admiration for the bravery of five children and a dog."

"Let's have a look then." Shaz tipped the envelope. The little skulls grinned up at them from the table, each with a figure five on its forehead. The children grabbed them and pinned them on their jackets.

Mickey called Raider to heel. "Here, you barmy mutt." He fastened the fifth badge to the dog's collar. "I hope you realize they don't

usually award this badge to dogs – they reckon you're a special case." He grinned, ruffling Raider's ears. "*Nut* case, if you ask me." He turned to the others, rubbing his hands together.

"Now then – who fancies a nice forty mile hike across the moors?" He ducked, chuckling, as a shower of small missiles came flying at his head.

READ ALL OF THE OUTFIT'S THRILLING ADVENTURES!

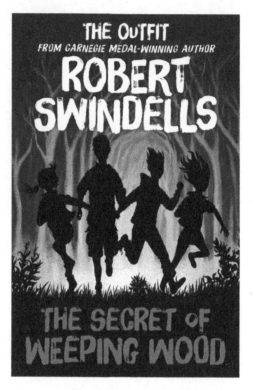

ISBN 978-1-78270-053-1

The Outfit had never really believed
the stories about the ghosts of Weeping
Wood – until now. But as they investigate
the mysterious cries, truth suddenly
becomes stranger – and more
terrifying – than fiction!

READ ALL OF THE OUTFIT'S THRILLING ADVENTURES!

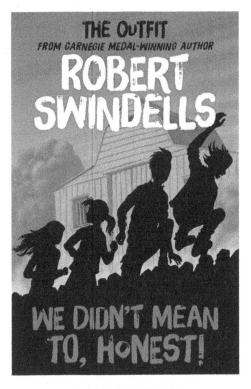

ISBN 978-1-78270-054-8

Miserable Reuben Kilchaffinch is going
to fill in Froglet Pond, and he won't let
anything, or anyone, get in his way.
The Outfit are desperate to save the pond
and its wildlife and they plan to stop
Kilchaffinch – at any cost!

READ ALL OF THE OUTFIT'S THRILLING ADVENTURES!

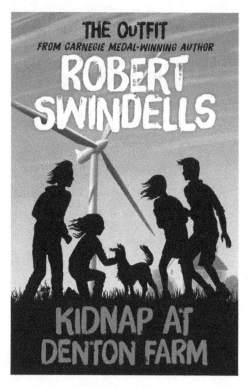

ISBN 978-1-78270-055-5

When Farmer Denton has a wind turbine built on his farm, little does he know what trouble it will bring. After one of them goes missing, The Outfit must solve the mystery of the malicious caller – and fast – if they ever want to see their friend again!

READ ALL OF THE OUTFIT'S THRILLING ADVENTURES!

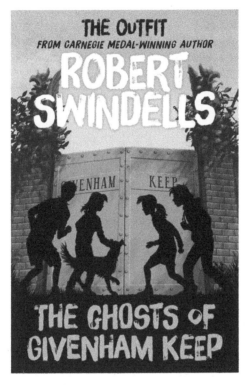

ISBN 978-1-78270-056-2

Steel gates and barbed wire have
been put up around the old mansion in
Weeping Wood. Someone has something to
hide and The Outfit intend to find out what.
But their innocent investigation soon
takes a sinister turn…

READ ALL OF THE OUTFIT'S THRILLING ADVENTURES!

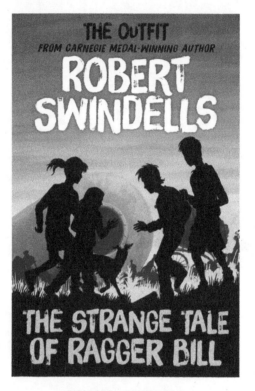

ISBN 978-1-78270-058-6

A little girl has gone missing and some
of the villagers are taking matters into their
own hands. Ragger Bill is the main suspect,
but The Outfit are sure he is innocent.
They must find the true culprit – and
fast – before things go too far!